Too timid to Talk

BONNEY
PRESS

Published by Bonney Press,
an imprint of Hinkler Books Pty Ltd
45–55 Fairchild Street
Heatherton Victoria 3202 Australia
www.hinkler.com

BONNEY PRESS

Illustration: Anna Shuttlewood
Text: Lisa Regan
Design: Bianca Zuccolo
Editorial: Zoe Antony

ISBN: 978 1 4889 3243 4

Printed and bound in China

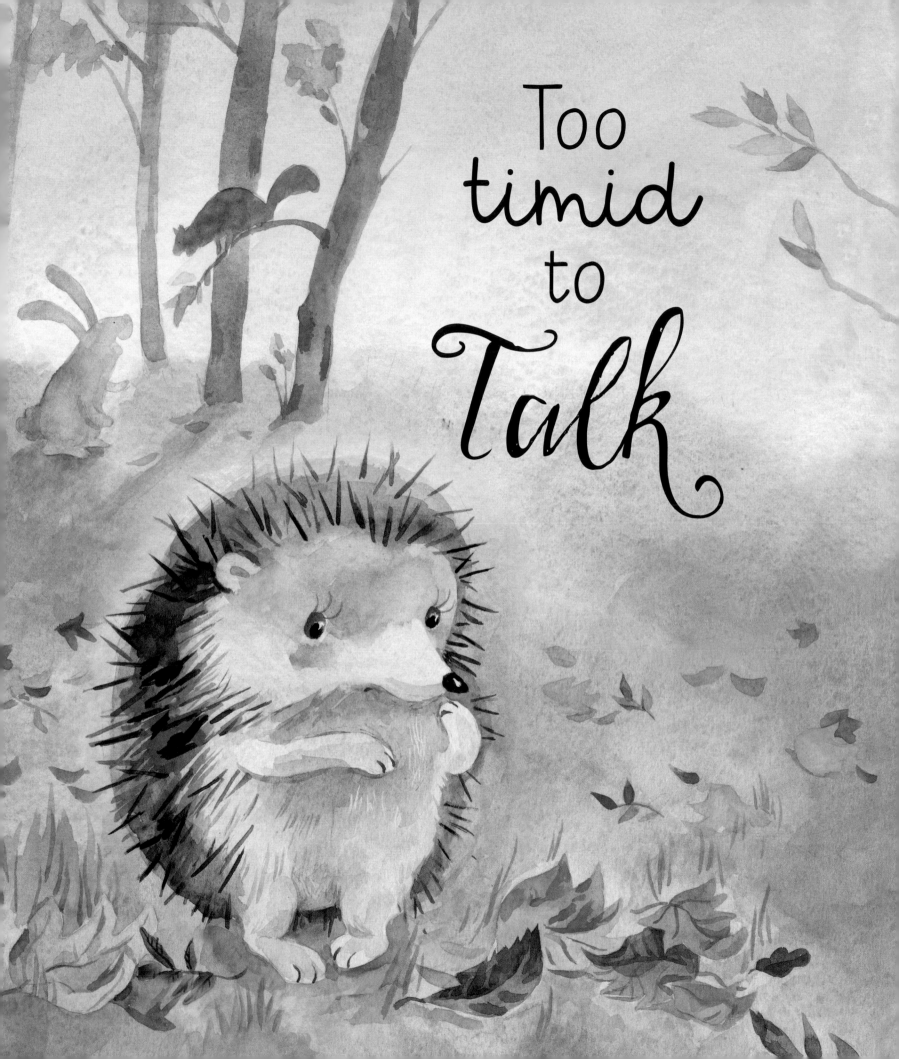

Too
timid
to
Talk

Today is a special day for Hedgehog. It is her birthday! Her tummy feels all trembly inside because she is so excited.

She would like to ask everyone in the forest to help her celebrate. They could have a party!

It would be a lot of fun, but she would need help to get everything ready.

Hedgehog trundles off to see who is around. The squirrels are running up and down the trees in a very busy way. They chatter loudly as they leap from branch to branch.

Hedgehog opens her mouth to ask for their help, but the squirrels look so focused! She gets a little nervous.

A tiny squeak is all that comes out.

Hedgehog scurries away. She catches sight of Bunny, who looks very busy indeed. He is gathering lots of food in his basket. Someone is going to have a feast today!

Hedgehog hides herself away and watches him work.

She is too scared to interrupt as he rushes around.

There is a lot of noise coming from the clearing nearby. Hedgehog tiptoes over and sees Bear pulling away fallen branches and sweeping up leaves.

Hedgehog loves Bear. He is so big and friendly.

She whispers, 'It's my birthday!',
but Bear doesn't hear her.

Hedgehog cheers up when she sees Frog blowing up balloons. Maybe he could spare a couple for her birthday party?

But Frog sees her and quickly hops away before she has the chance to speak.

'I suppose I am just too prickly for balloons,' she sighs.

Owl is perched in the branches, teaching her class to sing. They are practising a jolly tune at the top of their voices.

They all fall silent when they see Hedgehog listening below. She was going to invite them to sing at her party, but now she is too scared!

She burrows into a pile of leaves instead, until the owls fly away.

Hedgehog creeps towards the Deer family. They are shy and quiet like she is. Surely she can be brave and ask them for their help on her special day? Mummy Deer is busy giving directions as her children cluster around her legs.

But the deer hear the crinkle of leaves as Hedgehog approaches; they look up, startled.

Hedgehog feels awkward and decides not to bother them.

Then Hedgehog feels a strange trembling beneath her feet. Suddenly, Mole appears in a pile of dirt! He squints around, then sneaks out a piece of paper from underground and gives it to Deer.

Mummy Deer stamps her hoof on the middle of the paper, and Mole dives back down into the darkness.

Hedgehog wishes she was brave enough to talk to Mole, but she was too timid and now he's gone.

Hedgehog scurries away so fast that she almost crashes into Fox! They both jump in the air, and Fox drops a parcel he is carrying. He slides in front of it and puffs up his tail to hide it.

Poor Hedgehog gets such a fright that she squeezes her eyes shut tightly and curls into a ball.

Her heart beats faster as she tumbles away down the hill.

Little Hedgehog nearly rolls straight into the river! Luckily, she bumps into a pile of logs that stop her. As she uncurls, she sees Beaver.

He is eagerly gnawing a tree trunk into lots of smaller pieces. Hedgehog wants to ask him to come to her party, but she hesitates.

'Can't stop!' mutters Beaver. 'Lots more of these to make!'

A splashing in the river catches her attention. It is Otter, diving and tumbling in the water with his friends.

As Hedgehog watches them play, a tear trickles down her cheek. She wants to spend her special day with friends, too. But everyone is so busy and she is too timid to bother them and get in their way.

She picks her way out of the reeds and heads back into the trees.

Hedgehog's head hangs low as she wanders back home. She doesn't even see Badger as he joins her on her path.

'You look so sad,' he says. 'Can I help?'

Hedgehog stops and sniffs. 'I just needed a few friends to help prepare a small party for my birthday, but everyone's so busy that I didn't dare ask them.'

'It's ok,' comforts Badger. 'Come on, I'll walk you home and cheer you up.'

He parts the leaves at the edge of the clearing, then nudges
Hedgehog through the gap in front of him...

'SURPRISE!'

Hedgehog looks around in wonder.

The birds burst into a chorus of 'Happy Birthday' and all the other animals cheer. Fox trots forwards with a huge present and Mole has a card that everyone has signed. The Deer family have decorated a cake, and Bunny's feast is enough to feed all of them.

Bear has cleared a huge space for them to have a party and Beaver has gnawed enough seats for everyone. The forest is decorated with Frog's balloons, streamers hung by the squirrels and waterlilies collected by the Otters.

They are so fond of their prickly little friend that they wanted to make sure her day was extra special, even if she was too timid to mention it!

Hedgehog spins around gleefully. Her friends have worked so hard and made her so happy! She realises that her friends will always be there for her, no matter how busy they seem!

As she blows out her birthday candles, Hedgehog closes her eyes. 'I wish that I will never be too timid to talk, ever again!' And her friends promise that they will help her make that wish come true.